NICK® all grown UP!™

Coolest Girl in School

by Wendy Wax
illustrated by Artful Doodlers

D1125498

Ready-to-Read

Simon Spotlight/Nickelodeon
New York   London   Toronto   Sydney

KLASKY CSUPO INC.

Based on the TV series *Nickelodeon All Grown Up!*® created by Arlene Klasky, Gabor Csupo, and Paul Germain as seen on Nickelodeon®

SIMON SPOTLIGHT
An imprint of Simon & Schuster Children's Publishing Division
1230 Avenue of the Americas, New York, New York 10020
© 2005 Viacom International Inc. All rights reserved.
NICKELODEON, *Nickelodeon All Grown Up!*, and all related titles, logos, and characters are trademarks of Viacom International Inc. Created by Klasky Csupo Inc.

Manufactured in the United States of America
First Edition
2 4 6 8 10 9 7 5 3 1

Library of Congress Cataloging-in-Publication Data
Wax, Wendy.
Coolest girl in school / by Wendy Wax;—1st ed.
p. cm.—(Ready-to-read)
"All grown up."
"Based on the TV series All Grown Up! created by Arlene Klasky, Gabor Csupo, and Paul Germain as seen on Nickelodeon."
Summary: Angelica buys new clothes in an attempt to be more popular, but her friend Kimi is more successful when she decorates one of Angelica's hand-me-downs.
ISBN 0-689-86647-X (pbk.)
[1. Self-perception—Fiction. 2. Interpersonal relations—Fiction. 3. Clothing and dress—Fiction.]
I. All grown up (Television program) II. Title. III. Series.
PZ7.W35117Co 2005
[E]—dc22
2004013175

"Hey, Angelica," Kimi said.

"Do you want to go to the beach?"

"No, thanks," said Angelica.

"My mom is taking me shopping.

I need a new look if I am

going to be popular."

"What do you need for school?"

Charlotte asked.

"Let's see . . . ," said Angelica,

"I need four shirts,

three skirts, ten hair clips . . ."

Angelica tried on an outfit.

Jane Banks, the most popular girl

in school, giggled at Angelica.

"Mother," Angelica cried,

"I would never wear anything

so ugly," she said loudly.

Later, Angelica showed
her new clothes to Susie and Kimi.
"My goal this year is to be
popular," said Angelica.

"So do not feel bad if I stop
hanging out with you guys."
"Gee, thanks," said Susie and Kimi.

"What are these clothes for?"

Kimi asked.

"I am giving them away,

but you can take any

old rags you like,"

said Angelica.

Kimi took a light blue shirt.

At home, Kimi tried on the shirt.

The sleeves were too long,

and it was too plain.

Kimi had an idea.

The next morning Kimi

painted tiny roses

on the collar and cuffs.

Next she sewed on colorful buttons

and cut the sleeves.

Finally, the shirt was done.

Angelica spent Sunday evening
getting ready for the first day
of school.

"Hey, Jane, what's up?"
she practiced saying. She was
getting cooler by the minute!

Angelica was excited to wear her new
clothes on the first day of school.

"Where did you get that shirt?
I love it!" said a familiar voice.
It was Jane Banks!

"Thanks! I—" Angelica began,
but Jane was talking to Kimi.
"I rescued it from a junk pile
and gave it a makeover,"
Kimi said proudly.

"That is **my** shirt!" Angelica said.

But no one heard her.

"How much money do you want
to make me a shirt?" Jane asked.

"Five dollars?" Kimi asked.

"Great!" said Jane.

"I will take six shirts."

"Have you seen Kimi?" Angelica
  asked Susie.

"Yes," Susie said. "I love
  what she did to your shirt."

15

Angelica went straight
home after school.
She took out some markers,
an old skirt, and other supplies.
Then she got to work.

She drew on butterflies

and sewed on jingle bells.

Then she was done.

The next day, Angelica jingled
through the hall.
"It's not Christmas yet!"
a boy called after her.
Everyone, including Jane,
was laughing at her.

"I really like your jingly skirt,"

Kimi said.

Angelica did not answer.

"Sit here, Kimi!" Kimi heard

Jane say.

Kimi sighed and went over.

That night Chuckie asked Kimi
if she wanted to play chess.

"Sorry, Chuckeroo," she said.

"I have tons of homework
and six shirts to finish."

"Need some help?" asked Chuckie.

"Can you sew?" Kimi asked.

"No," said Chuckie. "But I can do your homework."

"Chuckazoid, you're the best!" Kimi said.

"Why are you up so late?"

Kira asked Chuckie.

"Homework," said Chuckie.

Kira saw Kimi's name on the page.

"Kimi will not learn a thing

if you do her homework," she said.

Chuckie gulped. "Sorry."

The next day was a school assembly.

Angelica saw Jane give Kimi a note.

Angelica read it.

It was an invitation to a barbecue.

Angelica had an idea!

"Are you going to Jane's barbecue?"
Angelica asked.

"No, I have to make shirts,"
said Kimi.

"You should go to put in a good
word for me," said Angelica.

"Why? I thought you were mad
at me, anyway," Kimi said.

"Please! It would mean a lot to me,"
Angelica begged.

Kimi agreed to go.

At Jane's barbecue,

Angelica hid in the bushes.

"Hey, Kimi!" called Jane. "Look!

We are wearing your shirts."

"You know, I got my first shirt

from Angelica Pickles.

"Isn't she great?" said Kimi.

"Not really. She is always trying to impress us," said Jane. "Angelica is fun and smart. You would like her if you got to know her," said Kimi.

"I am sorry you had to hear that,"
Kimi said to Angelica.

"It's okay," Angelica said sadly.

"Did you mean what you
said about me?"

"Yes," said Kimi.

Later that night Kimi stayed up
to finish making three shirts.
"It's past your bedtime," Kira said.
"The shirts can wait. Just finish your
homework—without Chuckie's help."
Kimi did as she was told.

"Are you having fun making shirts?"

Kira asked Kimi the next morning.

"It **was** fun, but now it's worse

than homework," said Kimi.

"You can always stop," Kira said.

"The kids will understand."

Kimi agreed!

Kira was right.

The girls did understand.

Kimi even gave them tips on

how to make their own shirts.

But Kimi had to make one last shirt.

Kimi gave Angelica the last shirt.

"Thanks!" Angelica said.

Just then, Jane walked by.

"Hi, Kimi! Hi, Angelica!" Jane said.

Angelica's eyes lit up.

Maybe this year she would

be one of the coolest

girls in school after all!